Christmas for Willy Redfern

a

Christmas in the Fandom Book

Christmas For Willy Redfern

Text copyright (Sweat of Brow) 2024 by Tallmadge Swartzfager

All rights reserved.

Published by Briny Bindings.

Printed POD by IngramSpark and affiliates, USA.

Author: Tallmadge Swartzfager
Editor: Tallmadge Swartzfager
Layout, Design, Formatting: Tallmadge Swartzfager

ISBN: 979-8-3305-6596-2

A Lamplighter Underground Book

Christmas for Willy Redfern

a
Christmas in the Fandom Book

Written by:
Tallmadge Swartzfager

Arras,
Northern France
*   *   *
# 24th December, 1916

"Right men!" barked an officer.

No one cared what his rank was, it was not high enough for it to matter beyond the mud and sludge of the trenches. He was the sort of man sent to bring in the brass monkeys on a cold day like this one. Oh, it was not his fault, he had not asked to be promoted to his petty, useless position. Still, the men looked away and tried to act busy, slipping into dug-outs and around corners as if they had somewhere to be.

"The line down to Albert was cut - haven't repaired it from the offensive. I need a man to take a message down there — on foot, by cart, horseback, I don't care — it has to be there tomorrow."

"Take it yourself," someone suggested.

"Whoever goes won't be expected back until the twenty-seventh," said the officer, ignoring the previous comment and waving a paper in the air, "and I have the leave-papers here."

"Oh, how lovely!" someone said loudly, "four day's leave for Christmas. Enough time to get out of earshot of the guns before you have to hurry back."

"I'll go."

The officer, disgusted but not surprised, had just turned to leave when the voice arrested him. "Ah!" he said, turning back around, "very good, corporal. This must reach Rawlinson, commanding the Fourth. And these are your papers — they'll keep you from getting shot. Well, getting shot by our own men anyways. There's a copy in French if you run into any frogs — blasted if I'm not fighting Huns beside Frenchies …"

"I'm expected back on the twenty-seventh?"

"Yes. You don't need to wait for a reply."

With that the officer left, muttering to himself about frogs and cold and pulling the collar of his coat closer. The men, having stayed still and preoccupied to avoid attention, now lept on the figure standing there with three packets of paper in his hands.

"Vibert, are you cracked?"

"Cracked?"

"It's nearly forty miles from here to Albert! You'll have to walk all night. Rawlinson and Gough just finished butchering our boys a month ago, and you're going to walk down there for your 'Happy Christmas'?"

"Yes."

"Jack! Jack! Get out here! Vibert's cracked!"

Jack appeared promptly, the crowd parting ways for him, and coming up to Vibert demanded, "What's all the hullabaloo about, boys?"

"Sergeant, Vibert's lost his mind. He's gonna carry a message down to Rawlinson in Albert with four day's leave. Haig —"

"God bless and keep the fieldmarshal and take him swiftly to his heavenly home!" sang out the men in ringing chorus.

"— was so sad to see them run out of men down there — they'll throw him against the Germans soon as look at him! No fresh bodies allowed in the Somme! And if the officers or the Germans don't get him, the lice will!"

"Yeah, remember poor John?"

"Poor John who went the blick home to his wife with all his body-parts intact and functional? Vibert, bring some lice back when you come and we can all get sick."

"No, you can't sacrifice Vibert to the cooties!"

"Gentlemen, please!" said Jack, "Vibert is going down to Albert and will be fine. There's nothing we can do to stop him, but give him his Christmas presents now and send him off."

Vibert grinned at his cousin.

"Are you mad, Jack?"

"He'll freeze!"

"He'll be shot!"

"Don't send him to the Somme!"

"I'm not going to the Somme," said Vibert, and confusion spread through the expressions of those present, "I'm going to visit my brother and my brother-in-law. They're stationed down there."

This changed things, and there were several jealous exclamations, cheers, jovial slaps, and much buzz of conversation.

"You lot!" came a thunderous shout and several of the privates went scattering. Another officer, with too much brass to fetch monkeys, stalked into their midst.

"Don't you know there's a war?" he barked, "you want to signal the Huns your position, serve 'em up a nice little tally of British soldiers mutilated by artillery — heh? Then get back to what you ought to be doing and not all standing in one place shouting and jumping around. This is Arras!"

"You think we'll be attacked?" Vibert said, and several privates near him inched away. "There hasn't been a December offensive by the Germans this whole war, not against Britain anyways."

"I suppose the Germans are all for peace this time of year," the officer stood toe-to-toe and face-to-face with Vibert, staring him down, "and I ought to let the men play football with them and sell them information in exchange for a few souvenirs? This is war, corporal, and there is no Christmas in the army."

Vibert did not flinch or blink, and after a moment the officer turned and stalked away again.

"There will be for Will Redfern," Vibert said suddenly, and the officer turned back sharply.

"And tell Willy 'Happy Christmas' for me," he spat.

Most everyone slunk back to their positions in the freezing pit they called home and a battle-front.

"I'm not comfortable with this situation," confided one of the men to Vibert, "I really think you'll be safer here."

"Doug, they won't actually throw me up out of the trench for the Germans to eat," laughed Vibert, putting a hand on his shoulder.

"No, I'm uncomfortable with the thought of you leaving the trench for Christmas," said Doug, "here you'd be safe if they shoot anything, not that I think they will. But out there, above ground, a random shell or a wandering plane with a bored pilot is all it takes and you're …"

"Douglas, I'll be fine," Vibert insisted, "egad, my boy, what has the war done to you that the trench is home? We need to get you out and about in the sun." Vibert was already walking down the trench to gather a few things and then head out. "When spring comes back to Arras, Doug, we'll —"

Two shells struck above the traverses, sending smoke and dust about, spraying everyone down with flecks of rock and globs of muddy snow. There were a few moments of confusion and slight panic before they confirmed everyone was alright, and then business went back to normal. Normal for a quiet day spent freezing at the bottom of a trench. Everyone quite forgot about spring returning.

Soon Vibert was off, his pack full of the gear he needed and a few things for himself and Bruce and Will when he found them — food, letters, extra socks, things like that. He went down Preacher Alley to the second line of trenches, up another winding passage to the third trenches, and eventually found his way to a place where there were no trenches, only roads across a scarred landscape and men moving up and men moving back.

Miles of lonely, muddy road stretched out before Vibert. The wreck of war lay all about him, and the stench and thunder of the front lines were his faithful companions. Here too the dead lay unburied: dead horses, burned trucks, shattered farm houses, spoiled barns.

Trees stood about like empty coat racks, whether defoliated by the bitter winds of autumn or the violence of war one could not tell. Streams, choked with mudslides and the wreckage of wood and steel, lay still and rank, dark and thick with filth and muck. The rutted road, with its long, thin pools of water, showed a reflection of the sky above like a glimpse peaked between the warped and knotted walls of an old barn. Up there an endless sea of silent grey rolled along, neither birds nor planes breaking its monotony. The only birds about were the ravens — and these, glutted with flesh, sat hunched in the skeletal trees, weary eyes gazing over the fields of the slain, too numerous for the already satiated and engorged ravens to keep up with.

Twilight was drawing near and Vibert was beginning to feel long hours of brisk walking. His pace had slowed, he knew, but he did not have strength to force himself to speed up again. Something caught his eyes, and pausing he squatted down. It was a locket, tacky with freezing mud and discoloured with blood. It had opened a crack, and Vibert flicked it with his thumbnail. Inside were two pictures - a mother and a young lady, a sweetheart or a younger sister. Probably dropped from the hand of a wounded soldier on a stretcher being loaded into the back of a truck or wagon.

A motor rumbled behind him and Vibert stood. A truck was coming, and he stepped off the road. The truck slowed and stopped.

"Where you from, mate?"

"Third, seventh division."

"No kiddin'! Hey, boys, it's one of Allenby's men! Where you headed?"

"Albert. I have a message for Rawlinson."

"Splendid! We're goin' down that way. Get in the back, we'll take you down."

Vibert walked around to the back. The men parted the canvas and gave him a hand up.

"I'm 'Enry," said one of the men with a smile, "where are you 'eaded?"

"Albert, same as you all I hear," Vibert answered, shaking his hand.

"Righto! We're the lucky blighters what get to go back. Just in time for Christmas too."

"Crap gift," retorted one of the other men.

"Watch your mouth Edward," Henry's genial face became stern, "and wish our guest an 'appy Christmas."

"What you got down in Albert?" asked Edward.

"Four day's leave to deliver a message, find my brother and brother-in-law, and then go back to Arras."

"You a doctor?" one of the other men asked.

"No. Why?"

"I've lost the skin off part o' me gums back behind me teeth, and it's kinda sore all down me throat. Thought you might know."

"How'd it happen?"

"Believe it or not his food was too hot," said Edward, "I think he burned himself. Lucky —"

"When we get back to Albert we'll get a doctor to look at it and if you *are* lucky you'll go back to Aire," Henry settled it, "don' disturb our guest with your bleedin' gums."

Edward chuckled.

"What?"

Edward looked at the fellow with the sore mouth, his eyebrows raising a little. "That was funny."

"How was it funny?"

"Well … it was a pun."

A mixed chorus of chuckles and disgusted sighs spread through the back of the truck. "He who would make a pun would pick a pocket," someone said. Edward shook his head and leaned back, crossing his arms across his chest. Henry glanced at him and grinned in one corner of his mouth.

They hit a particularly large bump in the already rough road and the men were tossed bodily into the air, ricocheting off each other on the way back down to the benches. Most of them were unphased, but the adventure elicited a string of muttered profanities from Edward and a comment about, "Like driving on a washer board." Henry looked at Vibert and gave a subtle shake of his head, rolling his eyes. A muffled shout of apology came from the front of the truck.

"What's that in your 'and?" asked Henry suddenly.

Vibert held it out and dropped it into his palm.

Henry turned it over, gently popped it open, examined it closely, and with a ragged sigh handed it back to Vibert. He looked out the back of the canvas, watching the scarred and muted countryside roll past. Vibert pocketed the locket and settled into his seat.

The conversations in the back of the truck were but whispered, and after a long day of walking, Vibert, now here able to rest his weary limbs, still warm from his exertions, rocking gently in the shelter of the canvas, began to doze off, head leaned back and eyes closed without his knowledge.

"Twilight of the gods."

Vibert lifted his head with a shake and squinted one eye open. Henry was gazing out the back of the truck, and quickly following his gaze he saw another of those thin, naked trees, its brittle branches full of drooping ravens, shadows barely visible in the last of the light.

"How now?"

"I wonder," said Henry, more to himself than in answer to Viberts question, "if those Huns think of that, when they see the trees full of ravens, too heavy to fly down for another meal … yet another meal … another feast!" His body convulsed with disgust. "Was the dragon of England the serpent that would eat Siegfried? Or Odin, shall he perish by the wolf that is the Imperial German Army? Shall they, when they have killed us all, find that they have consumed themselves as well? Man has made himself a god — a god of death, who has covered all the world in war, the final war, the great war."

Light, reddish and ghastly, flashed across the eastern horizon, glowing through the clouds. Artillery fire.

"I see it at night," Henry nodded, and all the men had now fallen silent, listening in rapt attention. "I see the fire and the ice — as the world was born, so shall it end, in smoke, poisoned smoke and a great rushing hiss of explosions as the freezing cold and the burning heat come from both sides … we shall all be surrounded, Britton, Hun, frog, on every side by death."

"But they that wait upon the LORD shall renew their strength; they shall mount up on wings as eagles; they shall run and not be weary; and they shall walk, and not faint. For the evildoers shall be cut off: but those that wait upon the LORD, they shall inherit the earth," quothe Vibert.

Henry smiled sadly. "You've read the legends too? You think there shall be an eagle that flies upon the wings of the morning up to the summit of that lofty mountain whence the healing waters flow like rain?"

Everyone looked at Vibert now. "God is not a man, that He should lie," Vibert shrugged. Even to him, the promises seemed far away.

"Aye, faith," echoed a voice, "and hope does not disappoint."

Then from a slight, silent form in one corner came the gentle music of a poem:

> "Long lays tell of many warriors:
> Heroes, princes, who, gods'-doom couriers,
> Messages brought of coming night
> When fire and water would claim the fight
> Of wolf and god, serpent and hero,
> Spawn of gods, sovereigns imperial;
> Bear-skinned champion, berzerker-strong
> Heirs embark to right sire's wrong,
> Mighty men in ancient hall
> Who long shall sleep before the Fall —

"Death of legend, faced the few;
Handful of heroes, hordes they slew:
Left behind treasures, kingdoms, men.
Twelve berzerkers, battle-harden'd
Sons of sire splendid, Angantyr,
Setting out to new adventure;
Death awaits by cursed blade:
Thirteen tombs in island's glade.
Now paths divide, tales diverge,
Of maiden Hervor and Chosen Sigurd.

"War with Huns, wars with Goths,
Great halls burning, gold hoard lost,
Mirkwood shadows, vast plain trembles;
Runes all written, dread-doom's symbols.
Long lineaged heroes to strife muster,
The Great War riding in gold lustre.
Now tell the tale, now sing the lay,
Of heroes bright in darkened day;
Haste the coda, quicken the end —
God-sired Chosen shall reign again."

"Sigurd won't do *us* much good, now will he, Ledge?" said Edward after a pause.

"Not Sigurd, Edward," corrected Henry, "there is another 'God-sired Chosen' who shall reign." He looked at Vibert. "One risen with healing in His wings."

Vibert delivered his message and was given a bunk in Albert that night. The next morning he went with a group of orderlies to the front, having been directed as to where he would find Bruce and Will's division. It was a wonderfully clear Christmas morning, the sun shining and snow all around. The clouds were gone, and it was so quiet one could almost forget.

Still, it was a miserable scene at times. Men and horses stood about freezing amidst the wreck of cannons, with nowhere to go and nothing to do.

Men would have been singing but the stern glares of their commanders warned them not to. Vibert kept asking for directions as he went and finally made his way down to the trenches where Bruce and Will would be.

"The Twenty-ninth? No. This is the Thirty-first. They're further south."

Apparently, someone had given him bad directions.

He made his way down the line, asking every so often if he had reached the Twenty-ninth. Finally he had, and he was directed to the regiment his brothers belonged to.

"I'm looking for Bruce Trevor and Will Redfern," Vibert was explaining.

"Will Redfern?" said someone, a faded and disheveled looking fellow who could have used a shave.

"Yes! Do you know him?"

"I don't think I will for long. The lieutenant is threatening to shoot him."

"What in heaven's name for?" Vibert has a mixture of fear, anger, and confusion.

"You remember that stunt we pulled a few years ago, when we were boys, the 'Christmas Truce' they called it. Will seems to think he can repeat that.

"Which I'm all for," the soldier gave a wide gesture with both his arms, "and if the krauts wanted to snipe him, they would have put a bullet in his skull already — but its the brass won't have it, 'course, have a war to perpetuate."

"Where are they?" Vibert nearly lept on the man.

"Down there," the soldier shook him off and waved him away, "I just came up myself. Just around a few traverses."

Vibert broke into a run. He came around a corner and knocked somebody into the mud. Shouts and curses followed him. When he passed the third traverse and had not found Will yet, he leapt up on the parapet and peeked his head over. There he was, half-way across no-man's-land, empty hands raised over his head, calling something. A few round, grey things moving about on the edge of the opposing trench told Vibert the Germans were listening but understandably nervous.

"If none of you will obey orders I'll shoot him myself and then court-martial the lot of you," snarled a voice, and turning, Vibert saw an irate officer waving his pistol at his men and fuming. No one moved.

"Fine then," said the officer, turning to a trembling private, "give me your rifle."

The poor soldier froze in terror, back up to the side of the trench, clutching his rifle to his chest.

Suddenly a string of oaths and phrases spoken so quickly Vibert could not understand them exploded from one of the other men, a big man. The big man stepped towards the lieutenant. The lieutenant's adjunct, a clean, polished, pallid, and sneering character with dark eyes pushed the fellow up against the wall, hissing threats. Vibert was distracted for a moment, and it looked like the soldier was going to punch the smarmy adjunct in the face when the long sharp tone of a whistle was heard and everyone involuntarily tensed.

Everything slowed, and Vibert saw the next seconds in exquisite, agonized detail. The confusion and fear in the men's eyes. The whistle falling from the officer's mouth and bouncing on its ribbon. The angry fellow's fist loosening and arm dropping, the sallow adjunct turning to look at his master. The barren fields of snow and razor-wire.

That whistle was supposed to signal attack, and after a split second of confusion, the soldiers realized what had happened. The Germans, hearing the note, panicked. Will, his pant leg caught in some razor-wire, froze and his eyes widened. Vibert screamed.

"William!!!"

A German machine gun nest roared to life suddenly. Will fell backwards with a jerk or two, lying sideways and half suspended in the air, his leg still caught on the wire. Vibert vaulted over the parapet.

Something tugged his ankle and he fell back with a curse. He kicked and hit nothing. He punched something solid and was slapped across the face and slammed into the trench wall.

"Vibert!" Bruce shook him, "Vibert! Stay down!"

"William!" Vibert screamed.

"You'll be shot!"

Vibert punched his brother again and then both instantly froze at the only German phrase they both understood.

"*Nicht schiezen, aufhören!* Don't shoot! Don't shoot!" someone was screaming from across no-man's-land.

The brothers leapt up and stuck their heads over the edge of the trench. The German and British lines were both silent. Suddenly a pair of hands appeared above the German trench, and a white cloth on a stake. After the hands came an officer. He stood on the edge of his trench for a moment. Vibert and Bruce watched him, sticking their heads up further.

The German let his hands down slowly and walked out with deliberate steps to where Will lay. He tugged his pants loose and picked him up.

"Don't shoot!" he called in perfect English, "I'm going to bring him over to you! Get a doctor!"

Then he carried Will. He picked his way around craters and barbed wire and came within a few yards of the British trench. Vibert, Bruce, and a medic jumped up and met him. They eased Will down to the ground gently.

Vibert looked over his brother-in-law quickly, and he knew. Another course for the ravens' feast.

"Vibert," Will gasped, his uniform soaked and riddled with holes, "Vibert!"

"Be still, it's alright, you're going to be alright," Vibert said, kneeling with one hand under Will's head and another around his shoulder, trying to hold him still for the medic.

"Vibert — it hurts!" Will cried, "Vibert — ah!"

The color was draining from his face rapidly and blood trickled from the corner of his mouth. The German was cursing and praying in English and in German. Bruce and the medic were trying to stop the blood flow, putting compression on Will's chest and abdomen.

"It's alright, Will," Vibert was pleading with a calm voice, trying to speak it into existence even as he comforted his young brother-in-law. "Bruce is gonna get you patched up, and we'll get you out of here, and then I've got a few things for you in my pockets — socks, new socks that Alfred's granny sent over, a note from Polly, a poem from Lucy, a —"

Will grabbed the front of Vibert's shirt and tried to pull him close with a trembling arm.

"Vi-ibert," he stuttered, his jaw clacking, "I'm … not … afraid!"

"You showed tremendous courage today," said the German suddenly, "peace sometimes takes more courage and valor than does war. You're a good man."

"Oh!" Will smiled a ghastly smile, blood in his teeth, dark rings around his eyes and his cheeks as white as sheets, "he's very nice, Vi — I think I'm dying, I can understand his German."

Vibert laughed and sobbed and grabbed his brother closer.

"No," Will continued, "I'm not afraid to die. I'm going home, Vibert — much sooner than you will be, or Polly and father and Kate —" he coughed, spitting blood across Vibert's face. "Agh! I'm going to see my Lord…"

"Will! Will, stay with me!"

"Vibert, it's alright, like … you said," Will sighed. The medic leaned back on his heels. Bruce kept trying to staunch the bleeding. He looked up at the medic and slowed down. The doctor shook his head, and Bruce stopped. "I tried … He knows," Will's shallow gasps stole away his voice. "Give thanks … to the Lord … He-his love endures … forever …"

Will's breathing slowed and they all bowed their heads. Vibert watched his eyes as the light began to fade.

"Ah!" Will tensed and his mouth opened in a silent cry of pain. "Vibert!" He relaxed and gasped.

"It's alright, Will, just like you said," Vibert said, "go to Him. I'll be right behind you."

Will laughed suddenly, and his lips formed, "P —" and then he was gone.

"Oh!" Vibert gasped back a sob.

No one else said anything. Vibert pulled Will into his arms, but he was already cold. Bruce put a hand on Vibert's shoulder.

"I'm so sorry," said the German.

"No," said Vibert, whiping away tears while still cradling Will's head in his lap, "it wasn't your fault. Or theirs," he added. "What's your name?"

"Addie von Wessermund."

"Vibert Trevor," he shook his hand, "my brother Bruce."

The German shook their hands, and then indicated Will. "May I?"

"Yes."

Addie reached over and shut Will's eyes.

"Sleep now," he said, then asked Vibert, "your little brother?"

"My brother-in-law," said Vibert, "I married his sister Polly."

The medic cast them all a glance and slid back into the trench.

"We have to go," said Vibert, trying to lift Will and sinking back to the ground.

"Here," Bruce said, helping him.

"*Frohe Weihnachten*, lieutenant," Vibert said, turning to Addie.

Addie saluted them. "Merry Christmas, boys."

"'Merry Christmas?'" asked Bruce as they slid back down into their trench.

"I think he learned English from an American," said Vibert.

Suddenly there was a crack of a rifle and Bruce and Vibert dropped to the ground. The greasy adjunct lowered his gun, chambered another round, and then raised the rifle again.

"What have you done?" Vibert cried, slapping the gun down.

Adolf von Wessermund stood stock still. He raised a hand to his chest, then to his eyes. Blood. Well, if that bullet had not gone right through him! He looked up from his hand to his trenches ahead of him. Hanz was there, staring at him, mouth agape in disbelief. Shot in the back.

Addie motioned for him to stay, and then as deliberately as he had walked out he walked back, collapsing over the edge of the trench. He landed in a heap, and immediately many hands pulled him up out of the mud and onto a shooting bench. Men were moving and shouting all around him. His captain was by his side in a moment.

"Wessermund you stupid fool!"

"Oh, come now, sir," he said weakly, "that's no way to —" he coughed.

"Save it — say something meaningful I can repeat to your father."

"I'm going to cross the river," Addie seized his arms, "and rest in the shade on the other side. Tell him that."

His captain nodded.

"The … papers," said Addie quickly, "you know the ones —"

"Yes."

"Ai. Hanz!"

The soldier came over, eyes wide.

"Write to Erica."

Hanz nodded.

"And my sister Heidi."

"Yes, lieutenant."

Addie reached out with the last of his strength and slapped Hanz across the face. "Don't 'Yes, lieutenant' me when I'm dying."

"Sorry Addie!" Hanz sobbed, falling across his chest.

"It's alright, Hanz," Addie winced.

"Why did you do it?" Hanz cried, grabbing his commander by the collar. The captain laid a gentle hand on him.

"I did the right thing, Hanz."

The captain pulled Hanz off gently, but Addie was already dead. Hanz sobbed and the captain put an arm around his shoulder.

"The best of last words," observed the officer, "noble and chivalrous."

"He was the best commander ever!" sobbed Hanz, burying his face in the captain's coat like a child.

"He knew what he was doing. A smarter man would have calculated the risks and stayed here," the captain soothed him and then pushed him away, stepping over to look down at Addie's face, "but a good man, a man of honor, would stand up and walk into death for what was right, would march into hell for the cause of heaven." He pulled his eyes shut.

Vibert watched Addie walk back to his trench with faltering steps and then collapse out of sight.

The adjunct handed the rifle back to the trembling private and walked over to the lieutenant. "Thank you, my lad."

"You —!" Vibert leapt upon him and slammed the adjunct against the trench wall.

"Easy does it, corporal," the lieutenant stuck his pistol next to Vibert's ear, "let go of him before anyone gets into trouble."

Vibert released him with a violent shove, and the adjunct straightened his coat with a disdainful glare.

"You shot a man in cold blood."

"We are at war, soldier, this isn't a football match," said the adjunct in a dry, bored tone of arrogance.

"Remember that, all of you," the officer said, as if he was giving a lecture at a university, "there is no Christmas in the army. We have orders to prevent fraternization with the enemy of any sort by any means. It is a matter of the security of military intelligence, and troop morale."

"You murdered this man's brother-in-law," said the big man from earlier, still cursing and speaking with a thick accent, "you could have held him here at gunpoint with your blasted pistol but you let him go up into no-man's-land because you're too much a coward to pull the trigger yourself and you wanted to make an example of him, use him as bait against the Jerries."

"He knew," the officer waved it away, "he disobeyed orders he should have followed, walked into no-man's-land, and was killed by the enemy. This is war, and he was a soldier —"

"He was a boy, lieutenant!" screamed Vibert and everyone jumped back and cowered. "He was sixteen years old!" he shouted with a sob, "he was a child!"

"This isn't a war, lieutenant," the big man stepped in, "it's Christmas. General Rawlinson will hear of this."

The lieutenant and his aide turned and left without a word.

None of the men spoke as Vibert and Bruce picked Will up in their arms and carried him away. They had not gone far before Vibert collapsed.

"Bruce!" he sobbed, "what have I done?"

"Vibert — nothing!"

"Will — Will is dead and it's my fault!"

"No Vibert, he was under my care. You weren't even supposed to be here."

"I could have jumped up as soon as I saw him there, called to him — I could have saved his life. Now I have to write the family and tell them he's dead — he's dead because I —!" He bit off each word in anger and started crying.

"Vibert, it happened too quickly," Bruce grabbed his shoulder, "I was right behind you. You were on that parapet a second before the whistle blew. I saw Will too — but I couldn't save him either. Or Addie."

So they both sat there and cried. Men walked by. Finally Vibert stood up.

"No," he said, taking a deep breath, "it hurts, but Will was right. The Lord was waiting for him. He was with him in no-man's-land, and He was there helping that German carry him, and He took him home — away to home, sweet home. We weren't going to save him, Christ did that. His grace was sufficient for Will even today. While he lived, his life was Christ's, and when he died — oh! what gain! what raptures of bliss!

"I could almost be jealous, except it hurts so much! But I will choose to trust God.... His life meant something, Bruce," Vibert's eyes stung with frozen tears, "and so did ... today."

Bruce stood too. "Let's get him out of here."

"Can we help?"

The brothers turned to see six men carrying a cot like a stretcher. One was the big man, another the trembling private.

"Please."

"Your brother meant a lot to us," said the big man when they had laid him on the canvas, "some of us didn't realize until he was gone …"

"He never stopped singing," said one of the men as they lifted Will onto the stretcher, "all through the Somme. Everyone else we knew was killed, but he kept smiling. He wasn't stupid, so I asked him where he found the joy to sing through bomb blasts and nights spent sleeping in gore. He told me about his hope. I knew all that already, but he kept smiling and singing. And I knew Jesus had to be more than what I'd always heard in church."

"I didn't know him long," said the trembling private as they all carried him, "but before he went over, he told me, 'It's Christmas. The Saviour is come, born as a babe to be the Lamb that was slain to conquer the world from sin and death. Now I hear the Lion roaring over the sound of the cannons, and He's' …" the private wiped away a tear and sniffed, "'He's calling me to be like Him.' Then, with the lieutenant screaming at him, he put a foot on the ladder and winked at me. 'It's Christmas,' he said again, 'the Saviour is come!' And then he went up whistling 'Let There be Peace on Earth.'"

"I would overhear to him telling the men about Christ," said the big man, "but I never really listened myself, if you understand me — kept distance between us with a screen of cigarette smoke. Until today … I was listening to him making his plan to go over, and heard him talking about the Lion and the Lamb. And I thought to myself, very suddenly, 'Now only a lion could scare away the wolves of war.' and then Willy said, 'He's calling me to be like Him.'"

"Last night," said a fellow with a dark complexion, long face, and hard features, "William was after me again - egad, he never shut up! I didn't want to hear any more about his Christ Jesus or the Gospel, and I told him so. 'I've heard everything you have to say about it,' said I, 'a hundred times since you first showed up. Now if you've got anything new to tell me about Jesus, say it once and then never mention it again or I'll make sure I'm behind you next time we go over!' He just looked me dead in the eye and said, 'He is like me.' It meant something last night, but it means more today."

"He wasn't a stupid kid," continued the big man, "he was a good man. I think he saved our lives. Let them know that, when you write home."

And so they brought Will up out of the trenches to that marred countryside where the land was bare and the air still. They buried him beside one of those lonely trees, and fashioned a cross out of scrap wood. The men returned to their trenches, leaving Vibert and Bruce alone. Quietly the wind blew down the plain. Raven feathers fluttered. Vibert bent and picked them up, looking down at them with a sigh. Then he pulled the locket from his pocket, stuck the feathers into the golden chain, and hung it from the cross.

"This is the promise: God-sired Chosen shall reign again," he said softly. "Happy Christmas, Will."